LOVE IS MY FAVOURITE THING

Emma Chichester Clark

For my two grandpas,
age 602 and 637
in dog years.

Emma Chichester Clark began the website **Plumdog Blog** in 2012, chronicling the real–life adventures of
her lovable "whoosell", (whippet, Jack Russell and poodle cross) Plum. Emma soon gained thousands
of loyal Plumdog devotees, and in 2014 a book of the blog was published by Jonathan Cape.
This picture book story is the first Plumdog book for children.

LOVE IS MY FAVOURITE THING
A RED FOX BOOK 978 1 782 95147 6

First published in Great Britain by Jonathan Cape,
an imprint of Random House Children's Publishers UK
A Penguin Random House Company

Penguin
Random House
UK

Jonathan Cape edition published 2015
Red Fox edition published 2016

1 3 5 7 9 10 8 6 4 2

Copyright © Emma Chichester Clark, 2015

The right of Emma Chichester Clark to be identified as the author of this work has been asserted in accordance with the Copyright, Designs and Patents Act 1988.

Red Fox Books are published by Random House Children's Publishers UK,
61–63 Uxbridge Road, London W5 5SA

www.randomhousechildrens.co.uk www.randomhouse.co.uk

Addresses for companies within The Random House Group Limited can be found at: www.randomhouse.co.uk/offices.htm

THE RANDOM HOUSE GROUP Limited Reg. No. 954009

A CIP catalogue record for this book is available from the British Library.

Printed in China

Penguin Random House is committed to a sustainable future for our business, our readers and our planet.
This book is made from Forest Stewardship Council® certified paper.

MIX
Paper from
responsible sources
FSC® C018179
FSC
www.fsc.org

I AM PLUM,
but I love being called Plummie.

And **LOVE** is my favourite thing.

I love all kinds
of weather,
especially wind.

But I don't
really like rain.

I love snow,

and I love sun.

I love my bear,

and my bed.

I love treats,

and
catching,

I love sticks
SO much,

BUT LOVE IS MY VERY FAVOURITE THING!

I love the park and my friends.
I love the grass and the trees.
I love it when Emma says, "Good girl, Plummie!"
when I do a poo, as if it's so, so clever.

I know it means she loves me
and **LOVE** is my favourite thing.

But yesterday, **EVERYTHING** went wrong.

When Emma said, "Don't go in the pond, Plummie!" I wasn't listening.

No, Plum!

I heard Rocket say, "Come on, Plum! Come on! Come on!"

Come back, Plum!

And I just couldn't help it.
I really couldn't.

Water is one of my other favourite things! I love it!
I LOVE it!

"Isn't this **great**?" said Rocket. And it was.
It really was...

...until
Emma arrived.
"BAD GIRL!"
she shouted,
and I knew I'd
made a **BIG** mistake.

She marched me home.
The whole world was **black**.
Will she still love me?

Sam and Gracie
heard what I'd done.
"Oh, Plum!" said Gracie.
"Oh, Plum!" said Sam.
Will they still love me?

I ran to find them
a present but...

...there was only a cushion.
When Gracie tried
to take it...

...I just couldn't help it!
I really couldn't. It's one
of my **favourite** games!

I love it! I LOVE it!
"No! Plum!" cried Gracie.

"No! No, PLUM!" cried Sam.
They were pulling and I was
pulling...

...Sam was shouting and I was flying
and SUDDENLY...

"PLUM!" shouted Emma.

"VERY BAD GIRL!" she said.

"OUT YOU GO!"
said Emma,
and I realised I'd made
a dreadful mistake.
"Oh, Plum!" said Gracie.
"Oh, Plum!" said Sam.

Will any of them
still love me?

It seemed like forever but finally we all went to
the park. It was sunny and bright and everywhere
I looked I saw tiddlers with ice-creams.
"Plummie," said Emma. "That's not for you!"

But I really love ice-cream. I know **all** about it.

I know what it tastes like and I love it!

I just LOVE it!

And tiddlers are **always** dropping things...

...they drop things **right** in front of me...

...and I just couldn't help it. I really couldn't ...so I grabbed it!

"PLUM!" cried Emma.
Then everyone was running
and everyone was chasing!

I ran to my house
and waited and waited.
I knew that I'd made
THE MOST ABSOLUTELY
AWFUL MISTAKE!

"Oh, Plum!" said Gracie.

"Oh, Plum!"
said Sam.

"Oh, Plum!"
said Emma.

"What will your daddy say?" said Emma. "What a **BAD** girl!" The children just looked at me.

They'd all had enough of me.

They marched me downstairs and sent me to bed.

My whole world was black.
I stared at the darkness. I knew they
wouldn't love me anymore.

Eventually, they came and opened the door.

"Well, Plum,"
said my daddy.
"Are you sorry?"
he asked.

And I was. I really was.
I'd do **ANYTHING!**
as long as they
still love me.

"BUT DO YOU STILL
LOVE ME?

DO YOU STILL
LOVE ME?"

DO YOU STILL
LOVE ME?"

"Oh, Plummie!" said Emma.
"Oh, Plummie!" said my daddy.
"We do love you!
But – you've got to get better
and do as you're told, and
BE A GOOD GIRL!"

So I do try to be good.
I don't always remember – I wish that I could.
I still make mistakes and I still love ice-cream
and swimming, but I know they love me.
They do! They really do!

AND THAT'S WHY LOVE IS MY
VERY, VERY, VERY FAVOURITE THING!